SIGIL™

THE
MARKED MAN

Sigil™: Allied Enemies Vol. 2, JUNE 2002. SECOND PRINTING. Originally published in single magazine form as **Sigil™** Vol. 1, Issues #8-#14, and **CrossGen Chronicles™** Vol. 1, Issue #4. Copyright © 2000, 2001, 2002. All rights reserved. Published by CrossGeneration Comics, Inc. Office of publication: 4023 Tampa Road, Suite 2400, Oldsmar, Florida 34677. **CrossGen®**, **CrossGen Comics®**, **CrossGeneration®** and **CrossGeneration Comics®** are registered trademarks of CrossGeneration Comics, Inc. **Sigil™**, the **CrossGen sigil™**, **CrossGen Chronicles™** and all prominent characters are ™ and © 2002 CrossGeneration Comics, Inc. All rights reserved. The entire contents of this book are ™ and © 2002 CrossGeneration Comics, Inc. The stories, incidents and characters in this publication are fictional. Any similarities to persons living or dead are purely coincidental. With the exception of artwork used for review purposes, none of the contents of this book may be reproduced in any form without the express written consent of CrossGeneration Comics, Inc. PRINTED IN CANADA.

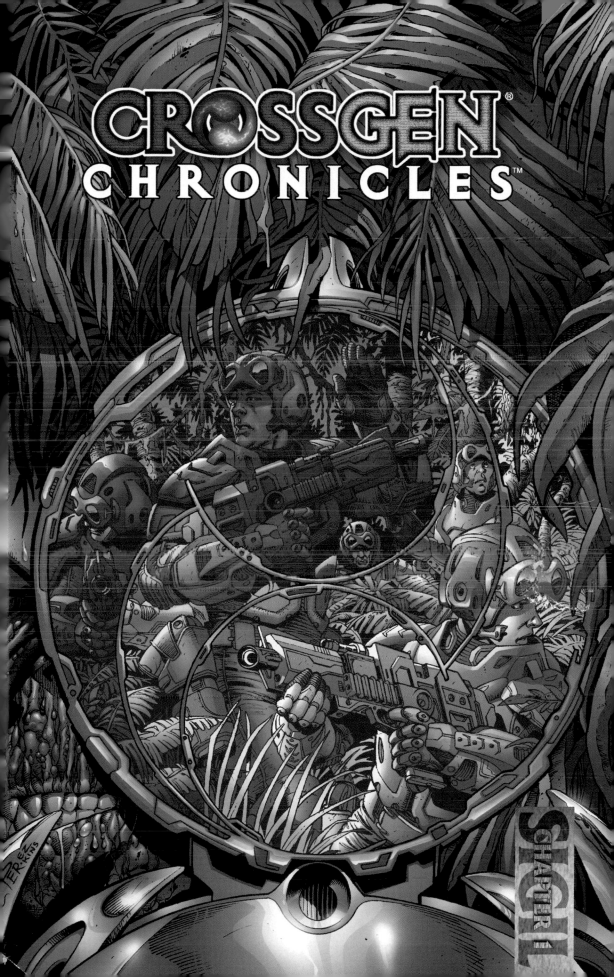

OUR STORY SO FAR...

The war between the humans and the Saurians has spread across three centuries and six planets, from Tcharun, the Saurians' homeworld, to the five human worlds of the Planetary Union. In between the warring nations is one small independent planet: the gaming world of Tanipal, ruled by the Sultan Ronolo.

SAMANDAHL REY

Former Planetary Union soldiers and best friends, Samandahl Rey and Roiya Sintor survived years of warfare only to become casualties of the war's economic devastation when their squad was deemed too old and too expensive to maintain. They came to Tanipal in search of work, which in Sam's case meant time spent at the illegal pseudosaur combat tables, controlling a mini-raptor fighter in battles to the death.

But greater danger was looming. The Saurian Prince Tchlusarud, secretly negotiating with the Sultan, had learned of Sam's presence on Tanipal. He ordered a Saurian commando team attack. During the raid, Roiya was mortally injured and Sam was given a strange brand on his chest, a sigil that turned out to link him to a source of amazing power. Roiya died...but not completely. Her essence became a part of Sam's ship, the *BitterLuck*.

ROIYA SINTOR

Sam discovered, after an explosive activation, that he had the power to reshape inorganic matter, absorb great damage, and even survive unprotected in vacuum. That initial explosion left the Sultan's guards, the humans, and the Saurians all believing that Sam had a new weapon – one they'd all kill to possess.

JeMERIK MEER

On the run from everyone, joined by Zanniati, the runaway wife of Tanipal's Sultan who guards a bigger secret; JeMerik, a Sultan's guardsman with a hidden agenda; and a pseudosaur stowaway, Sam and Roiya try to stay one step ahead of their pursuers. They have lived through Sam's encounter with the hunter Trenin of the First who disappeared, leaving behind his technologically amazing ship; Zanni's capture by Tchlusarud; her rescue by the seemingly unkillable JeMerik; Roiya's near-disassembly by Saurian technicians; and Sam's grudge match against Tchlusarud.

ZANNIATI

During their escape from Tcharun, to save the damaged *BitterLuck* (and its sole occupant, Roiya) from destruction at the hands of the Saurians, Sam, directed by a strangely emotional JeMerik, does the only thing he can to save Roiya: merge both ships together. Now Roiya is a part of the mysterious Trenin's ship, but alive.

That's the situation *now*. Ten years earlier, as Roiya remembers it...

TCHLUSARUD

THERE ARE CERTAIN DOWNSIDES TO BEING DEAD.

Oh, DON'T GET ME *WRONG*. THERE ARE ALSO *PLUSES* TO BEING... WHAT, A GHOST IN THE MACHINE...?

I GOT TO TRADE THE EVENTUAL RAVAGES OF *OLD AGE* FOR A PERKY SET OF TACHYON THRUSTERS AND THE PERMANENT CURVES OF A STARSHIP CHASSIS.

AND UNLESS SAM DECIDES IT'S "FUNNY" TO PROGRAM GRAY HAIR INTO MY HOLOMATRIX, NO ONE WILL EVER CALL ME *GRANNY*.

BUT I'D BE LYING IF I SAID I DIDN'T MISS THE WORLD OF THE TACTILE. OF THE LITTLE FLESH-AND-BLOOD PLEASURES THAT MEANT THE WORLD TO ME FRESH OUT OF BOOT CAMP...

...LIKE THE TASTE OF A CRUNCHPUFF BAR...

...OR THE RECOIL OF MY FIRST CLACKRIFLE...

...OR HOW IT FELT TO GRAB A PITCHER OF SUDS AT THE BLASTER BAR...

SO, OUT OF *RESPECT*, THAT WAS *IT* FOR THE *BRAWLS*...WHICH WAS A REAL *SHAME*...

...BECAUSE THAT WAS THE MOST ACTION *ANY* OF US HAD SEEN SINCE *ENLISTING*.

THREE MONTHS *LATER*, JUST AS I WAS CONSIDERING TAKING UP *NEEDLEPOINT* FOR THE *THRILL* OF IT...

WE *FINALLY* GOT A *MISSION*.

SAM?

C'MON, SAM! WE'RE LATE FOR THE BRIEFING!

YOUR CHRON'S FAST. WE'VE GOT FIVE MINUTES. BE RIGHT THERE.

BACK THEN, NONE OF US WERE SURE WHAT TO MAKE OF SAM. HE WASN'T *SHY*, HE WASN'T A *JERK* -- HE WAS JUST *DISTANT*. KEPT TO *HIMSELF*.

WHICH, OF COURSE, EVERYONE TOOK TO MEAN THAT HE *WAS* A JERK, BUT AT THE END OF THE DAY...

...BUT I'M GETTING AHEAD OF MYSELF.

DON'T LET ME HOLD YOU *UP*.

'S'OKAY. CRUNCH-PUFF?

NO, THANK YOU.

RIGHT. WOULDN'T WANT TO GET COURT-MARTIALED FOR FRATERNIZING, WOULD YA?

FUNNY. LET'S *GO*.

WHY *NOT*? NOTHING *INTERESTING* KEEPING US *HERE*.

SAM'S *QUARTERS* WERE AN EXTENSION OF WHAT WE LAUGHINGLY CALLED HIS *PERSONALITY*: NEAT. ORDERLY.

TIGHT.

AND *DEADLY DULL*.

AWRIGHT! GIMME SOME OF THAT SWEET, SWEET COMBAT...

Um...≳MUNCH≲... WHERE ARE THEY HIDING THE REST OF THE PLATOON, FARQUAR?

DUNNO. WHATEVER THIS IS, THEY'RE KEEPIN' IT SMALL. JUST A FEW MISSION SPECIALISTS LIKE YOU AND ME... AND REY, THERE...

...RASPLEY, TOWMAZEE, RILEH AND HASTON.

'SUP.

HEY, I THINK I HEAR SOMEBODY COMING...

KCHUNK

HERE WE GO...

PLACES, PEOPLE. WE GOT A LOT TO COVER.

SGT. GRANNART... WHAT'S THE NEWS ON SGT. WHILTS? ANY WORD YET?

THERE IS...

...BUT YOU'RE GOING TO BE SORRY YOU ASKED.

LIGHTS.

<HE WILL *NOT* FOUL THIS DAY, MOTHER.

<NOT *THIS* DAY.>

<TCHUXXAN, YOUR *OTHER* SIBLINGS ONLY *BARELY* MAINTAINED THEIR TEMPERS WITH YOU THROUGH THE YEARS.

<IF YOU EXPECT *TCHLUSARUD* TO DO *LIKE- WISE...*

<...YOU *MAY BE SURPRISED.*

<YOU'RE *WELCOME* TO PUSH YOUR BROTHER IN WHATEVER DIRECTION YOU *LIKE--*

<--BUT BEAR IN MIND THAT IT'S THE *CORNERED ANIMALS* WHO FIGHT THE *FIERCEST.*>

<THEN FIGHT HE SHALL, MATRIARCH. THERE IS SOMETHING *OUT* THERE.>

<THANK YOU, HUNTGUIDE. EVERYONE STAY *HERE.* <I WILL RETURN WITH THE *KILL.*>

<JUST *REMEMBER,* BROTHER... *INSECTS* DON'T *COUNT.*

<*HAR!*>

I'M *IMAGINING* THE *CONVERSATION,* OF COURSE.

WITHOUT *TRANSLATORS,* THE MEANING WAS... *LOST,* SHALL WE SAY.

NO DOUBT ABOUT IT.

FACHOOM

WE WERE IN *TROUBLE*.

HOLY %*@!! I THOUGHT WE WERE SUPPOSED TO BE CRASHIN' A *RELIGIOUS* CEREMONY!

HATE TA SEE WHAT THEY'RE PACKING WHEN THEY'RE *NOT* IN CHURCH!

BRAKOW BRAKOW

SO MUCH FOR OUR *AMBUSH*!

I'M THINKIN' UNION INTELLIGENCE NEEDS TO WORK A LITTLE *HARDER* NEXT TIME, REY!

AGREED. ATTACKING DURING A SAURIAN CEREMONY MADE *SENSE*...

...BUT MAYBE SOMEONE SHOULD HAVE TOLD US THEY'D *BE* CARRYING *HUNTING* WEAPONS?

AAAAH—

TOWMA!

NO!

BEFORE I COULD *BLINK*, THERE WERE CASUALTIES ON *BOTH* SIDES.

THEY'D GOTTEN THE *MATRIARCH* OUT OF THERE *IMMEDIATELY*--

--BUT THERE WAS STILL PLENTY OF THE *ROYAL BROOD* AROUND--

BACK *ATCHA*, PUSBAG!

-- AND TCHLUSARUD WAS LOSING *FAMILY* WITH EVERY PULL OF A *TRIGGER*.

FOUR HUNDRED YEARS WE'VE BEEN AT WAR WITH THE SAURIANS.

FOUR *CENTURIES* DURING WHICH WE'D MADE LEAPS IN TECHNOLOGICAL PROGRESS AND CULTURAL ACHIEVEMENT...

FOUR CENTURIES DURING WHICH WE'D ADVANCED UP THE *EVOLUTIONARY LADDER*...

...ALL OF WHICH COUNTED FOR *NOTHING* THAT DAY.

THAT AFTERNOON, WE WERE JUST *MAMMALS* AND *REPTILES*...

...BURNING AND BLEEDING...

...AND PRAYING TO GODS WHO PROBABLY COULDN'T HAVE CARED LESS.

RIIILEH!

I REMEMBER BEING *SHOCKED* BY SAM'S *OUTBURST.* *"I'LL BE DAMNED,"* I THOUGHT. *"HE DOES HAVE A HEART!"*

"RIGHT?"

SHE'S *DEAD.*

OF COURSE SHE IS, SINTOR.

SHE WAS *DEAD* THE MINUTE SHE MADE THIS ABOUT *REVENGE.*

SHE *FORGOT* THE MISSION *OBJECTIVE.*

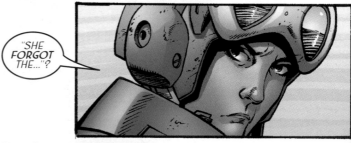

"SHE *FORGOT* THE..."?

FORGET *YOU.*

HURRY!
HE'S GETTING
AWAY!

I SEE
HIM!

WHAT? I
CAN'T HEAR
YOU!

I SAID,
I SEE HIM!
HE'S --

I NO LONGER
REMEMBER WHICH
STRUCK US *FIRST:*

A RASP LIKE
BONES BEING
DRAGGED
ACROSS
PAVEMENT--

I'M--WAIT--ING,
HU--MAN--ZZ.

Ck COMME--
AN--GGET
MEEE.

--OR THE DEAFENING DIN
OF *FALLING THUNDER.*

TO THE SHIP.

WHAT? BUT, SIR--

I SAID, TO THE SHIP!

LET'S GO!

--HADDIM RIGHT WHERE WE--

--MY KID SISTER'S BRAVER THAN--

--FEEL LIKE PUKIN'. HAD A RIFLE, I'D TAKE MY SHOT ANYWAY...

WOULDN'T DO YOU NO GOOD, FARQUAR. UGLY DONE RUN OFF ALREADY.

TRUE. TCHLUSARUD'S BROTHER WAS NOWHERE IN SIGHT.

WHICH LED US TO BELIEVE WE WERE HOME FREE...

...BECAUSE WE'D FORGOTTEN ABOUT TCHLUSARUD *HIMSELF.*

HE HAD SAM IN HIS SIGHTS. SADLY, FOR TCHLUSARUD...

CLOCK IS *TICKING,* PEOPLE! *HUSTLE!*

ME?

WERE YOU THERE, SINTOR?

YOU LISTEN TO ME, YOU IDIOTS! YOU'RE ROLLING OVER ON THE MAN WHO KEPT YOU ALIVE BACK THERE!

EVERYONE LOVED WHILTS. EVERYONE WANTED BLOOD!

BUT IN CASE YOU DIDN'T NOTICE, WE WERE AT A %*@#! WATERFALL!

IN CASE YOU DIDN'T NOTICE, THE RIVER WAS WAY TOO FAST TO CROSS!

WE COULDA--

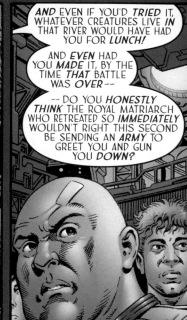

AND EVEN IF YOU'D TRIED IT, WHATEVER CREATURES LIVE IN THAT RIVER WOULD HAVE HAD YOU FOR LUNCH!

AND EVEN HAD YOU MADE IT, BY THE TIME THAT BATTLE WAS OVER--

--DO YOU HONESTLY THINK THE ROYAL MATRIARCH WHO RETREATED SO IMMEDIATELY WOULDN'T RIGHT THIS SECOND BE SENDING AN ARMY TO GREET YOU AND GUN YOU DOWN?

SAMANDAHL REY GOT US OFF TCHARUN 'LIVE. PERIOD. EAT THAT-- AND KEEP YOUR MOUTH CLOSED WHILE YOU'RE CHEWING.

IT WAS A GOOD SPEECH. DID THE JOB. NO ONE SAID A WORD THE REST OF THE WAY HOME.

PROBLEM WAS, EVEN THOUGH I KNEW I WAS RIGHT, THERE WAS NOBODY TO CALM ME DOWN.

I WAS STILL WORKED UP.

YES, SAM MADE THE RIGHT CALL. YES, HIS DETACHED NATURE, HIS COLDNESS, SAVED US ALL--

--BUT WITHOUT ONE REGRET?

WITHOUT ONE CROSS WORD FOR THAT SAURIAN BASTARD?

GOOD LORD -- HOW COLD WAS THAT MAN?

YOUR POINT *BEING*...?

THAT WHEN PEOPLE CALL SAM *INSCRUTABLE,* IT'S REALLY NOT A *COMPLIMENT?*

THAT WE *REALLY* NEED SOME *PLASMA WEAPONS?*

THAT THE NEXT TIME SAM TEASES YOU BY FEEDING HALF A CRUNCHPUFF TO THE *PSEUDOSAUR,* YOU'RE GOING TO PLUNGE OUR SHIP INTO A *WHITE DWARF STAR?*

NO. NO.

YES.

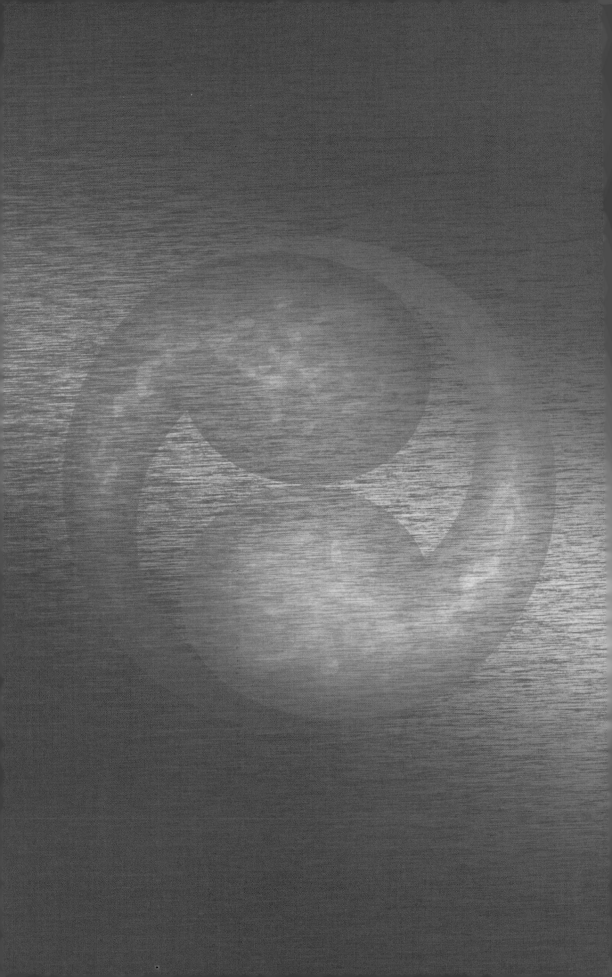

SO SHE'S DONE IT.

BEING DISINHERITED WILL JUST MAKE TCHLUSARUD A BIGGER PROBLEM.

THE PRINCE WAS ON THE VERGE OF BECOMING A HUMAN ALLY, AND NOW THIS.

I THOUGHT HE WAS GETTING CHUMMY WITH THE SULTAN?

THAT WOULD HAVE BEEN NEGATED IF OUR BUTCHER HAD DONE HIS JOB.

AS IT IS... WE'RE BACK TO SQUARE ONE.

WE'VE LOST GROUND WITH THE SAURIANS, THE SULTAN, AND THE COLONY WORLDS...

...AND NOW WE'LL HAVE TO BEAR THE EXPENSE OF AN ASSASSINATION SQUAD TO ELIMINATE THIS STUPID NUISANCE...

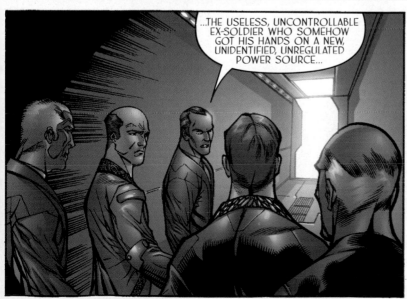

...THE USELESS, UNCONTROLLABLE EX-SOLDIER WHO SOMEHOW GOT HIS HANDS ON A NEW, UNIDENTIFIED, UNREGULATED POWER SOURCE...

...SAMANDAHL REY.

NO THANKS TO YOU RUNNING OFF TO PLAY GLADIATOR WITH LOSER...

BUT, ROI --

I DID IT FOR YOU. I GAVE HIM ALLA YOUR LOVE...

...THEN MADE HIM FEEL YOUR PAIN.

YEAAUGH! SPEAKIN' OF, *WATCH* IT WITH THOSE CLAWS, YOU LITTLE MONSTER!

ROI, YOU GOTTA TRAIN THIS THING BETTER...

WHA--?

TRAINING'S FOR THE SOLID PEOPLE, SAM. HE'S ALL YOURS.

I EVEN NAMED HIM AFTER YOU...

...TROUBLE.

SAM?

TROUBLE?

JOKE?

ARF YOU THERE, SOLDIER?

Huh?

Oh. YOU'RE A RIOT, ROI.

HEY -- IS HE HOUSETRAINED?

SO... ZANNI...

YOU GOTTA HELP ME MAKE A COURSE DECISION HERE.

SEE, ROI AN' ME, WE HAIL FROM THE HOMEWORLD, BUT OUR FAMILIES RAN OUTTA ROOM FOR US AN' WE NEVER NAILED RESIDENCY PERMITS OF OUR OWN.

TANIPAL'S A BAD IDEA, WHAT WITH THE SULTAN ORDERIN' OUR DEATHS AND ALL...

THAT'S WHERE YOU'RE FROM, RIGHT, MEER?

Oh...NOT ORIGINALLY...

BUT I DON'T THINK I SHOULD GO BACK TO WHERE I CAME FROM.

GAIA'S OUT. TANIPAL'S OUT.

OF THE COLONY WORLDS, THAT LEAVES DELASSIA, ZANNI'S WORLD, AS OUR MOST LIKELY SAFE HARBOR.

Gaia

Victor

Kayseecay

DELASSI∤

Tcharun

Tanipal

Brejhur

HOW 'BOUT IT, ZANNIATI? YOU MIND IF WE MAKE CAMP ON DELASSIA?

I... ah...

DON'T YOU WANT TO GO HOME?

"WELL, YES-- BUT DELASSIA HAS SO LITTLE TO OFFER YOU."

"S'OKAY. LITTLE'S 'BOUT WHAT WE NEED."

TANIPAL:
PLANETARY
UNION
EMBASSY

PRNNG

INCOMING MESSAGE LOGGED.

PRIORITY RED.

PERSONAL CODA ATTACHED.

INCOMING MESSAGE LOGGED.

PRIORITY--

SHUT UP.

IDENTITY: RONOLO IV,
SULTAN OF TANIPAL

STATUS: ALLY, TENTATIVE
SEE ALSO: VESPER ACCORD
SECURITY ALERT 21-02

I WISH TO MAKE A FORMAL COMPLAINT TO THE PLANETARY UNION.

THE SAURIANS HAVE JUST INFORMED ME THAT MY WIFE *ZANNIATI* HAS FLED TCHARUN IN THE COMPANY OF THE OUTLAW *SAMANDAHL REY.*

PRNNG

ENTER AUTHORIZATION FOR CODA.

TAKE CARE OF IT, GAENA. QUICKLY AND COMPLETELY...

...THE VESPER ACCORD AND MY CONTINUED SPONSORING OF YOUR PLUSH EMBASSY ON TANIPAL ARE RIDING ON MY SATISFACTION IN THIS MATTER.

OOOOH! ZANNIATI AND SAMANDAHL REY!

WHAT ARE YOU TWO *DOING?*

*UN*DOING TWENTY YEARS OF DELICATE NEGOTIATIONS! DON'T MAKE ME GO HOME TO GAIA, YOU TWO...

...YOU'LL *PAY.*

"ZANNI, WE'RE HERE. WANNA GIVE US A TOUR?"

"WELCOME TO DELASSIA. THIS IS *IT.*

"DELASSIA WAS IN THE PROCESS OF BEING COLONIZED WHEN THE UNION HALTED THE PROGRAM...

"...ONLY HALFWAY THROUGH CONSTRUCTION.

"WE HAVE MINOR COLONY STATUS AS A RESULT OF OUR NOT BEING ENTIRELY SELF-SUFFICIENT.

"MOST OF THE ENGINEERING TROOPS ABANDONED HERE PUT DOWN ROOTS AND STAYED TO SALVAGE WHAT THEY COULD OF THEIR TERRAFORMING WORK.

"THEIR SIDELINE, FIXING AND RETROFITTING SHIPS FOR GAIA AND THE OTHER COLONIES, BECAME THE BASIS FOR OUR ECONOMY.

"DELASSIA'S RICH WITH NATURAL RESOURCES, BUT THE EQUIPMENT TO MINE THEM IS STILL BEYOND OUR MEANS.

I'M NOT SUPPOSED TO BE COMING HOME...

...SO I'M NOT SURE HOW I'M GOING TO BE RECEIVED.

HEY, IF THEY GOT A PROBLEM WITH YOU COMING HOME, THEY GOT A PROBLEM WITH ME.

THAT'S NICE, SAM.

GO.

EXPLORE.

EXPLAIN.

KICK TAIL.

DON'T WORRY ABOUT ME...

I'LL JUST STAY HERE AND WATCH THE SHIP.

WHY?

WHY NOT COME ALONG?

JeMERIK, YOU'RE TALKING TO A HOLOGRAPHIC CONSTRUCT TIED TO THIS PROJECTOR.

I CAN'T JUST DECIDE TO LEAVE...?

OKAY, MAYBE I'M NOT LOOKING SO GOOD... SCARED THE PSEUDOSAUR.

GRAWWWR

WE'RE GONNA NEED A LEASH FOR THAT CRITTER. WE CAN'T HAVE HIM SPOOKING THE LOCALS.

'CAUSE THAT WOULD BE **MY** JOB.

I'M THE GHOST, RIGHT?

C'MERE, YOU!

WHOOPS!

RIGHT. I'M THE GHOST.

OH, WELL.

I DON'T FALL THROUGH THE DECK--I CAN'T TOUCH YOU.

STILL ONE STEP BETTER THAN BEFORE, EVEN IF IT DOESN'T MAKE SENSE.

IT DOES MAKE SENSE...ENERGY HAS LIMITS...

ASSUME YOUR SYSTEM PERMITS A LIMITED PHYSICAL INTERACTION. HAVING AUTO-PLANE ORIENTATION ALLOWS A PSYCHOLOGICAL RELATIONSHIP TO "NORMAL" THAT--

JeMERIK...

THERE'S NO NEED FOR JARGON.

NOBODY ASKED FOR AN EXPLANATION.

JUST HOW MUCH *CAN* YOU DO?

ZANNIATI, I REGRET HAVING TO SPEAK TO YOU SO IN PUBLIC.

I KNOW...

WAIT, YOU TWO.

KLEK

NOW WE CAN SPEAK FREELY.

MOM! DAD!

WELCOME HOME, BABY GIRL!

ZANNI!

COULD YOU HAVE BEEN COLDER TO ME OUT THERE?

DON'T BE SILLY. I DON'T HAVE TO EXPLAIN POLITICS TO YOU.

OH, MY POOR LITTLE ATI-ATI! I HEARD HE HURT YOU?

WE'RE SO PROUD OF YOU, PRINCESS. THE SACRIFICES YOU'VE MADE FOR ALL OF US HERE...

Oh, SWEETIE, WE MAY HAVE BEEN AGAINST YOUR IDEA, BUT TELL US--

--WAS IT WORTH IT?

I WON'T LIE AND SAY IT WAS THE BEST OF EXPERIENCES, BUT I KNEW WHAT I WAS GOING TO DO WHEN I DECIDED TO MARRY RONOLO.

...YOU KNOW ME...

SO IF YOU'RE ASKING DID I ACCOMPLISH WHAT I'D HOPED TO...

"WITH THE ECONOMY OF THE ENTIRE PLANETARY UNION FAILING, IT WAS CLEAR THAT THE NEEDS OF THE YOUNGEST AND POOREST COLONY WORLD WERE GOING TO BE OVERLOOKED.

"DELASSIA'S ECONOMY IS LARGELY CENTERED ON SHIP REPAIR.

"WE HAVEN'T YET BEEN ABLE TO SET UP AN EXTRACTION OPERATION LARGE ENOUGH TO TAKE ADVANTAGE OF THE NATURAL RESOURCES THIS PLANET OFFERS--

"--TOO EXPENSIVE.

"I WAS YOUNG, RESTLESS, DESPERATE TO BE ANYWHERE BUT HERE BUT UNWILLING TO JUST ABANDON MY HOME.

"I LOVE SHIPS, AND THERE'S NOT ONE I CAN'T PILOT WITH THE BEST, BUT AS THE ONLY CHILD OF THE PRESIDENTS, DELASSIA NEEDED ME TO BE A POLITICAL ADVANTAGE, NOT A HOTSHOT.

"WE'D BEEN STRATEGIZING WITH ONLY THE UNION IN MIND WHEN *TANIPAL* PRESENTED AN OPPORTUNITY

"THE SULTAN RONOLO WAS SEEKING NEW AMUSEMENTS, AND HE'D SEEN A HOLO OF ME.

"HE OFFERED A *VERY* ATTRACTIVE BRIDEPRICE.

"TANIPAL WAS THE WAY STATION BETWEEN THE UNION WORLDS AND THE SAURIAN HOMEWORLD.

"SOONER OR LATER, *EVERYONE* COMES TO TANIPAL.

"HAVING AN OPERATIVE STATIONED THERE COULD ONLY HELP US MAKE IMPORTANT POLITICAL CONTACTS AND MARRIAGE TO RONOLO WOULD GIVE ME ACCESS INSIDE THE PALACE..."

DELASSIA: COLONIAL HEADQUARTERS.

...SO I PURSUED DELASSIA'S INTERESTS IN THE MOST OLD-FASHIONED WAY -- BY MARRYING FOR GAIN.

I TOLERATED RONOLO'S ABUSE UNTIL I HAD TO GET OUT...

...YOU KNOW THE STORY FROM THERE.

NOT THAT WE *APPROVED* OF WHAT OUR DAUGHTER WAS DOING...

...BUT SOMETIMES THERE'S NO STOPPING HER.

ZANNI DECIDED THAT THIS WAS HOW SHE WAS GOING TO BEST SERVE DELASSIA, AND SHE TURNED OUT TO BE AS INTUITIVE AS EVER.

AND SINCE IT GOT HER OUT OF THE PILOT'S SEAT, IT SEEMED ULTIMATELY *SAFER*...

ALTHOUGH, IF WE'D KNOWN OF THE *BEATINGS* SOONER...

NOTHING WOULD HAVE CHANGED. I HAD A *MISSION*...

ZANNI, YOU LED US AROUND LIKE A HOUND ON A BAITED SCENT TRAIL AN' ALL BUT LIED TO ME!

JUST HOW'RE WE SUPPOSED TO TRUST ANY OFFER *YOU* MAKE?

SAM... THE GREATEST SACRIFICE IS WHEN YOU HAVE NOTHING TO GIVE BUT YOUR OWN LIFE.

SOME GO TO WAR AS SOLDIERS.

SOME FIND *SUBTLER* WAYS TO WAGE WAR, SUCH AS GOING OFF TO A NEW PLACE AND PRETENDING TO BE WHAT YOU'RE NOT.

MARRYING FOR POSITION, NOT LOVE.

THINK ABOUT IT, SAM.

SAMANDAHL REY, MAY I SPEAK TO YOU *PRIVATELY?*

NNH?

SNAPPT

HREEEENK

WHO *DARES*?

I'LL GUT YOU FOR THIS INSUL--

YOUR PRIDE HAS BEEN BATTERED, PRINCE TCHLUSARUD, BUT YOUR WARRIOR'S INSTINCTS ARE UNHARMED.

YOU NEEDED TO KNOW THAT.

WEAPONSMASTER?

I AM NO PRINCE.

MY ELDER HAS DENIED ME THAT TITLE.

NEVERTHELESS, TCHLUSARUD, YOU ARE STILL AN ABLE WARRIOR...

"...TOGETHER WE WILL GUARANTEE HIS DESTRUCTION."
WELL, DOESN'T THAT BEAT ALL...

ONLY T'GIVE HER PEOPLE A SHOT AT A BETTER LIFE. YOU AN' I BOTH KNOW HOW HARD THINGS WERE ON GAIA.

LOOK AROUND. IT'S PRETTY FAMILIAR SURROUNDINGS HERE.

YOU HEARD HER SAY IT -- THEY GOT RESOURCES, BUT NO ACCESS.

ROI, WITH THIS POWER, I DO HAVE SOMETHIN' TO OFFER.

JUST A LITTLE HELP COULD MAKE A BIG CHANGE AROUND HERE.

DO YOU SEE WHAT I'M SAYIN'? THERE'S A BIG NEED HERE, AN' I'M GONNA GIVE 'EM A HAND.

WHAT?

YOU'RE NOT GONNA *CHARGE* THEM FOR THE PRIVILEGE?

WHO ARE YOU AND WHAT HAVE YOU DONE WITH "ALL FOR ME" SAM REY?

IT'S A GREAT IDEA, SAM AND I'VE GOT ANOTHER THOUGHT...

...I WONDER IF WE CAN USE OR CLONE THE TECH ON OUR SHIP?

IF I CAN OVERCOME MY SHOCK AT SAM'S GENEROUSITY ENOUGH TO CONCENTRATE... THAT'S GONNA BE TOU--

WHA--?

COME IN, ROIYA. YOU DON'T NEED TO HIDE.

WHO...

NO, *WHAT*...

...ARE YOU?

ONE WHO CAN BE BOTH MANY AND ONE!

AT THE MOMENT, JeMERIK MEER, FORMER SULTAN'S GUARDSMAN AND NOW MENTOR TO A SIGIL-BEARER...

...BUT I'M AFRAID YOU CAN'T SHARE THAT LAST PART WITH ANYONE.

AND YOU ARE THE WOMAN WHO IS ENDANGERING MY PLAN.

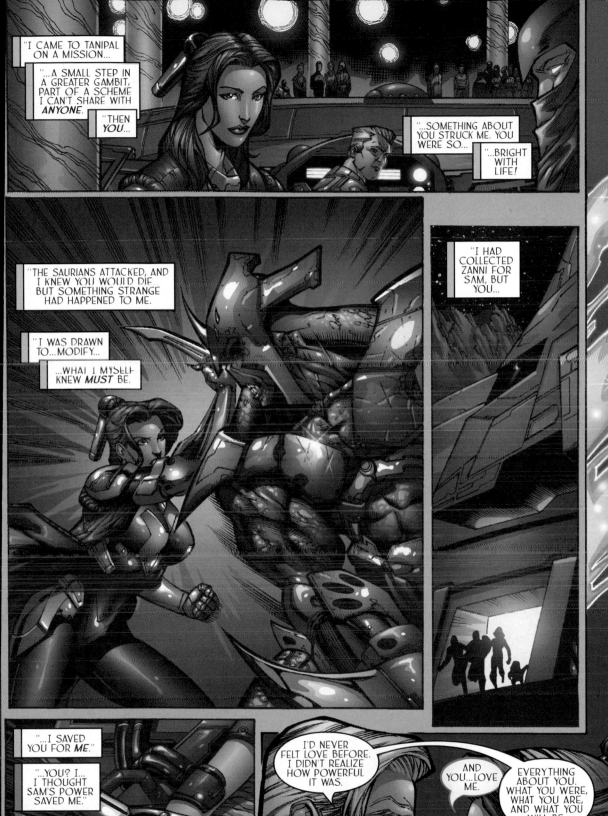

AND DO I HAVE TO...

...LOVE...

...YOU?

THAT'S TOTALLY UP TO YOU.

I GUIDE, I DON'T CONTROL.

ROIYA, EVERYTHING HAS A REASON, BUT...

JUST TRUST THAT I WOULD NEVER DO ANYTHING TO HURT YOU OR SAM.

SO, IN OTHER WORDS...

..."TRUST ME," HE SAYS.

TRUST YOURSELF...

...YOU KNOW HOW TO FIND WHAT YOU'RE LOOKING FOR.

THE KEY TO A TECHNOLOGICAL ADVANTAGE IS HERE.

THE ONE WHO CAN ACCESS IT IS YOU.

"I MAY BE A LITTLE MORE THAN HUMAN...

"...BUT SO ARE YOU."

CHAPTER 4

AND YOUR ANSWER IS...?

TCHARUN AGREES TO SUPPORT YOUR ASSERTION OF TANIPAL AS THE NEW SEAT OF HUMAN GOVERNMENT.

WE WILL ASSIST YOUR EFFORTS TO OVERTHROW THE CURRENT UNION WITH SHIPS, TROOPS, AND WEAPONS.

BUT WE WANT THE COLONY WORLDS BREJHUR AND KAYSEECAY GIVEN OVER TO US FOR SAURIAN EXPANSION...

...WITH THEIR HUMAN POPULATIONS INTACT.

COLONY WORLDS?

I ASSUMED YOU WOULD WANT THE PRIME WORLD... GAIA.

THROUGH INGESTION, WE HAVE LEARNED MUCH ABOUT YOUR KIND.

WE HAVE GAINED LANGUAGE, SCIENCE, AND ART.

WE DESIRE A BROADER SELECTION OF INPUT AND EXPERIENCE. COLONISTS HAVE OFTEN *EXPERIENCED* MORE THAN YOUR CROWDED CITY DWELLERS.

INGESTION...?

OUR SHIP'S BEING PREPPED AND WILL BE READY BY THE TIME WE BOARD.

YOU *ARE* READY TO LEAVE?

HUH?

HE'S GOIN'?

I NEED JeMERIK TO GO WITH ME...

...FOR PROTECTION...

...AND BECAUSE I'M AFRAID TO LEAVE HIM HERE.

PROTECTION?

I COULD PROTECT YOU JUST FINE!

CHAPTER 5

KEEP GOING, SAM.

GET IT TO YOU IN A MINUTE.

JeMERIK... ...WHAT'S WITH THIS?

COULDN'T YOU JUST FLAP YOUR ARM AND ZAP THEM OUT OF THE SKY OR SOMETHING?

AND IF I COULD, WHAT WOULD SAM LEARN FROM THAT?

"WELL, HE MIGHT LEARN TO *COUNT*.

"HE HASN'T NOTICED YET THAT HE'S BEEN GONE FOR HALF AN HOUR...

"...AND THAT PACK'S ONLY GOOD FOR TEN MINUTES OF THRUST.

"WHICH DOESN'T SEEM TO BE SLOWING HIM DOWN.

"LET'S JUST HOPE NOTHING GETS PAST HIM--

"-- OUR TEAM DOWN THERE'S GOT *NO* DEFENSE."

AS YOU HAVE SERVED THE ARTS OF COMBAT FAITHFULLY...
...IT PLEASES ME TO SHARE SOME MEASURE OF MY POWER WITH YOU!
HRAEEEEEENK!
WEAPONSMASTER
NO MORE. FROM THIS TIME ON, I HONOR HIM WITH THE NAM OF A GOD OF OLD--
KHYRADON
SERVE ME WELL AS TCHARUN'S CHAMPION. FIND THE HUMAN WHO WOULD THREATEN HER AND DESTROY HIM.
AS YOU WISH, GODDESS!
KHYALHTUA BE PRAISED!

CHAPTER 6

WELL?

HIGHER. WHAT AM I LOOKING FOR, AGAIN?

THE *GAMMA SENSORS.* PICTURE A CLUSTER OF *RIDGED METAL TUBING.*

I BET YOU SAY THAT TO *ALL* THE GIRLS.

GOT IT. POUR ON THE *JUICE* SO I CAN SOLID UP AND I'LL MAKE THE *ADJUSTMENTS.*

THERE. DONE AND *DONE.* TELL SAM AND ZANNI I CAN MEET *UP* WITH THEM NOW.

THEY'RE GONNA NEED ALL THE HELP THEY CAN *GET* RUNNING THE GANTLET PAST THE SULTAN'S *ASSASSINS.* COMING?

I HAVE SOME FINAL *TWEAKS* TO MAKE. IF ZANNI AND I ARE GOING TO "BORROW" THE SULTAN'S SHIP TO GET TO *GAIA,* I WANT ITS CLOAKING CAPACITY *DOUBLED* -- AT *LEAST.*

WHOSE OVERSIGHT *WAS* THAT?

Data unavailable.

=SIGH=

Download 72%

VERY WELL. TELL ME ABOUT THIS *"ROIYA."* SHE'S A *SPECTER* OF SOME SORT...?

ROIYA SINTOR 〖detail〗

During the skirmish 〖crossref〗, Sintor was slain by a Saurian warrior only moments after Rey received his sigil.

Though he was as yet unaware of its potential, his overwhelming grief nevertheless caused it to emit an explosive energy...

...which put a decisive end to the battle.

〖more〗

ROIYA SINTOR
[detail]
[continued]

Shortly thereafter, said energy was presumed to have merged Sintor's consciousness with selfship's computers...

...enabling Sintor to manifest her mental essence inside a mobile holographic construct.

"THAT'S...DISTURBING. I IMAGINE HER *CORPSE* IS ROLLING OVER IN ITS *GRAVE*."

Negative. Sintor's carbonform remains aboard this ship in stasis until such time as a reunion of body and mind can be engineered.

YOU DON'T *SAY*.

Download 100%

YOU'VE PROVEN QUITE THE *HEADACHE*, SAMANDAHL REY. WHEN YOU PROVIDED ZANNIATI *PASSAGE* FROM *TANIPAL*...

...YOU TOOK SOMETHING OF TREMENDOUS IMPORTANCE *AWAY* FROM ME.

I THINK IT'S TIME TO RETURN THE *FAVOR*...

"--BY SHOOTIN' UP *BYSTANDERS!*"

ALL RIGHT! ALL *RIGHT*, DAMN IT! *YOU WIN!*

NO, SAM! DON'T PUT *YOURSELF* IN HIS SIGHTS! THAT'S WHAT HE *WANTS!*

ZANNI, I *GOTTA* DRAW HIS *FIRE!* WORK WITH ME! I CAN *DISTRACT* HIM...BUT HERE'S WHAT I NEED *YOU* T'DO...

I CONFUSE YOU...BUT THIS IS NO RUSE.

I TRUST YOU NO MORE THAN YOU TRUST ME...YET IN ORDER TO DEMONSTRATE MY SINCERITY, I APPROACHED YOU WITH TOTAL VULNERABILITY.

RELEASE ME AND I VOW YOU NO HARM.

HIS SHIP'S EMPTY, SAM. THERE'S NO AMBUSH WAITING FOR US. I SAY WE HEAR HIM OUT.

AND THEN TAKE HIS SHIP.

NO!

YOU'RE MAKING DEMANDS? HE'S MAKING DEMANDS.

MOCK ME IF YOU WISH, SAMANDAHL REY. WE WILL SEE HOW HARD YOU ARE LAUGHING ONCE I FINISH MY TALE.

MERE DAWNCYCLES AGO, THE GODDESS KHYALHTUA APPEARED BEFORE HE WHOM YOU KNOW AS THE WEAPONSMASTER-- MY MENTOR--

TALK TO ME! WHY ARE YOU *FADING*? WHAT'S *GOIN' ON*?

LIKE I *KNOW*? SAM, *NO* ONE'S SURE JUST WHAT THE RELATIONSHIP IS BETWEEN THIS *HOLO-FORM* AND MY *PHYSICAL BODY* AND *YOUR SHIP* AND -- AND --

DISTANCE PLUS *TIME AWAY*, POSSIBLY? I'VE NEVER BEEN THIS FAR *REMOVED* FOR THIS *LONG*...!

COULD BE YOU'RE...*ADAPTING*. I'M *REACHING*, I KNOW, BUT STAY *CALM*! MAYBE IT'S JUST *TEMPORARY*!

WHAT IF IT *ISN'T*, SAM? *WHAT IF IT'S NOT*?

WE *NEED* YOUR *SHIP BACK*, SAM! TELL *LOSER* TO MOVE *FASTER*!

IMPOSSIBLE -- BUT *UNNECESSARY*. I HAVE THE *BITTERLUCK* IN *VISUAL RANGE*.

GOOD *NEWS*.

NOT *COMPLETELY*.

SEE FOR *YOURSELF*, SAMANDAHL *REY*. NOTE HOW *QUICKLY* IT CLOSES IN ON THE SMALLER CRAFT *AHEAD* OF IT. IS THAT--?

DAMN IT! IT'S *HER*!

HE'S GOT *ZANNI TARGETED*--

--AND WE'LL NEVER *INTERCEPT* IN *TIME*!

WE GOTTA *WARN* HER! RADIO! WHERE'S YOUR *RADIO*?

DIDN'T *YOU HEAR ME?* WHICH ONE OF THESE IS--?

IT DOESN'T *MATTER!*

THE SULTAN IS BROADCASTING A *JAMMING FREQUENCY* TO PREVENT HIS PREY FROM CRYING FOR *HELP*.

"WE HAVE TO *OPEN FIRE!*"

Detecting SAURIAN SHIP in PURSUIT.

SAURIAN? ALL THE WAY OUT *HERE?* IN A *NEUTRAL ZONE?* WHY WOULD IT BE TRACKING *M--*

REY.

IMAGINE. HE ACTUALLY FOUND *TRANSPORTATION...*

...FOR WHATEVER GOOD IT WILL *DO* HIM. THE *SHIELDS* ON THIS SHIP ARE ABSOLUTELY *ASTOUNDING*.

TELL ME, ARE THOSE *PLASMA TORPEDOES* I HEAR?

Affirmative.

AH.

"FOR A MOMENT THERE, I THOUGHT IT WAS *RAINING*."

SAM...?

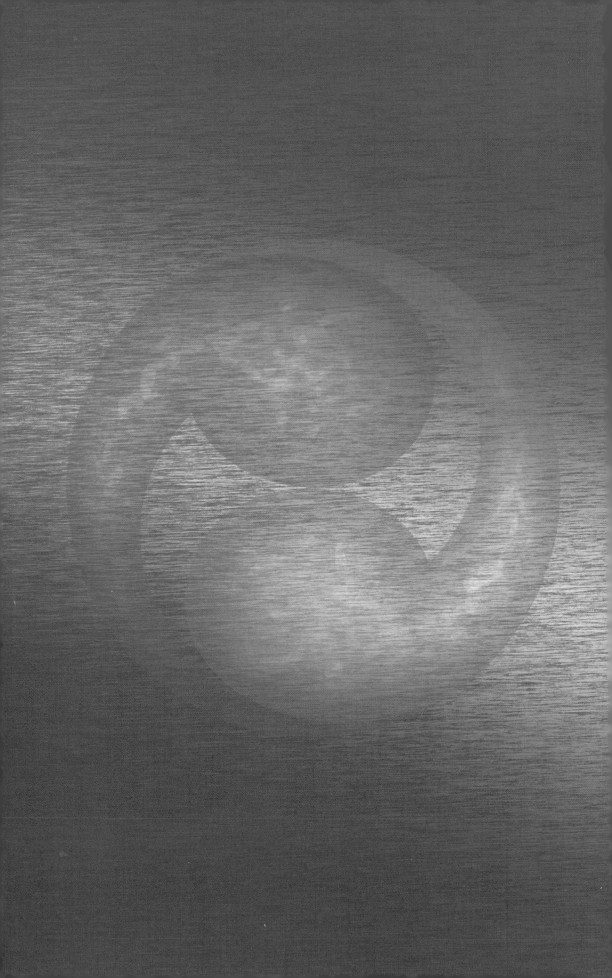

"THEY'RE OUR SHIPS."

--AND IT'S HEADED *THIS WAY!*

INCOMING!

FAWHOOM

WELL...

...*THAT* WAS A SHORT FLIGHT.

HOLD ON! THERE'S SOMETHIN' *MOVIN'* IN THE *WRECKAGE!* IT'S-- IT'S--

YOU. WHERE'S THE *SULTAN?*

--IT'S A *GUY* WITH A *BAD HAIRCUT?*

FREEZE!

NO.

SEE, *THIS* IS WHY I NEVER STOP TO ASK FOR *DIRECTIONS. WHERE* IS

THE *SULTAN?*

I *RESCIND* MY EARLIER *JUDGMENT.* YOU SEEM QUITE *PROFICIENT* IN YOUR *PILOTING* ABILITIES...

...FOR A *MAMMAL.*

WE'RE STILL *ALIVE,* THANKS TO *SAM.* I'LL LEAVE IT TO *YOU* TO GET PAST THE *SEVERELY THINNED FLEET.* YOU'RE NOT BAD AT THIS *YOURSELF...*

...FOR A *REPTAUR.*

RONOLO!

TRANSCEIVER *AMPLIFIED...*RE-ROUTING THE SIGNAL THROUGH THE NEAREST *UNION CRAFT...*

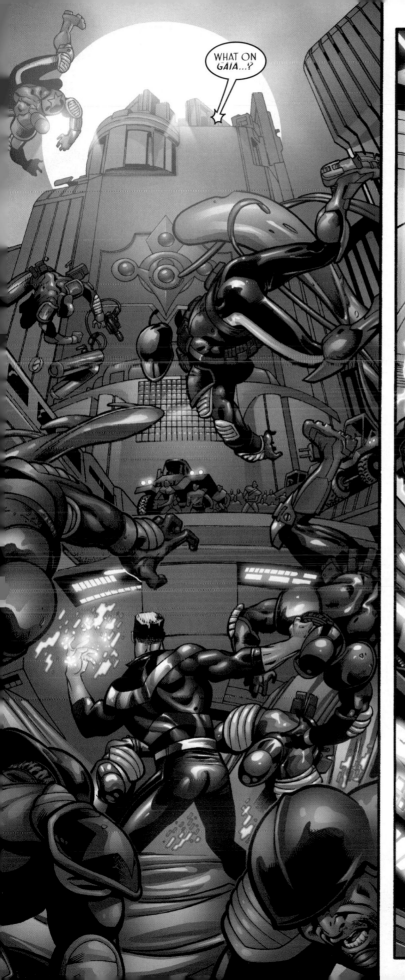

...NT, ...MY ...'S ...WN

I'M PROMISED IT WILL SOON BE UNDER CONTROL, RONOLO!

YOU HAVE **NOTHING** TO **WORRY** ABOUT!

SIR! YOU'RE RECEIVING A **PRIORITY** CALL!

GIVE IT **HERE!** IN THE **MEANTIME,** TELL SECURITY TO **BARRICADE** THE--

"--DOORS."

SKRAACHOOM

--REPEAT! THIS IS AMBASSADOR **ZANNIATI ORIBATTA,** IDENTITY CONFIRM CODE 727-THETA GAMMA!

THIS **SAURIAN CRAFT** IS UNDER **MY** CONTROL AND I COME IN **PEACE!** THIS CRAFT WAS COMMANDEERED IN **DESPERATION** IN ORDER TO DELIVER THE **DELASSIAN WARPDRIVE--**

--DESPITE SULTAN RONOLO'S **VERIFIED ATTEMPTS** TO **DESTROY** THE PROTOTYPE AND **MURDER ITS MESSENGERS** WITH HIS **OWN** HANDS!

MISTER PRESIDENT, I *IMPLORE* YOU TO CALL *OFF* YOUR ATTACK AND FOCUS ON THE *TRUE* ENEMY! GRANT ME *AUDIENCE*--

--AND I CAN DELIVER *DIRECTLY* TO YOU *INCONTROVERTIBLE EVIDENCE* THAT THE SULTAN IS *WHOLLY* AND *REPEATEDLY* GUILTY--

--OF *CONSPIRING* AGAINST THE *PLANETARY UNION!*

BTHAM

I HEARD *THAT.* BUT Y'KNOW *WHAT,* MR. PRESIDENT?

I AM *PERSONALLY* TAKIN' THE RESPONSIBILITY OF *PUNISHMENT* OFF YOUR *HANDS*--

--BEFORE THAT *RAT COWARD* GETS *AWAY* AGAIN!

STOP *RIGHT THERE!* I PROMISE YOU THIS MAN ISN'T GOING *ANYWHERE*-- NOT *NOW.*

TRUE. HOWEVER...

...YOU ARE.

NO!

C'MON, GROUND! MORPH! MORPH!

MORPH!

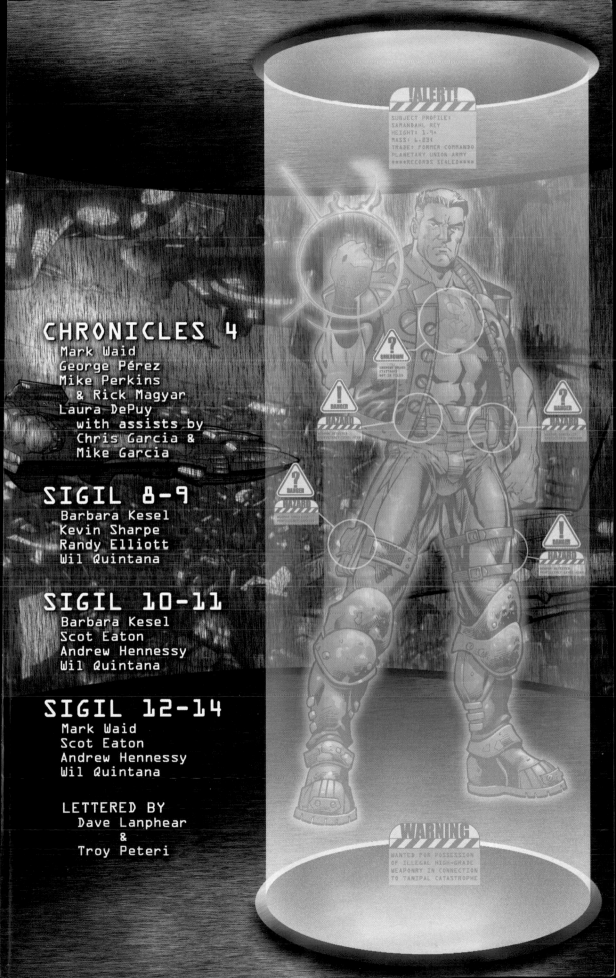

!ALERT!

SUBJECT PROFILE:
SAMANDAHL REY
HEIGHT: 1.9+
MASS: 6.23t
TRADE: FORMER COMMANDO
PLANETARY UNION ARMY
RECORDS SEALED

WARNING

WANTED FOR POSSESSION
OF ILLEGAL HIGH-GRADE
WEAPONRY IN CONNECTION
TO TANIPAL CATASTROPHE

The
CrossGen
Universe
created by
Mark Alessi &
Gina M.Villa

Mark Alessi
Publisher & CEO

Gina M. Villa
Chief Operating Officer

Michael A. Beattie
Chief Financial Officer

Tony Panaccio
VP Product Development

Chris Oarr
Director of Marketing & Sales

James Breitbeil
Director of Marketing & Distribution

Ian M. Feller
Director of Corporate Communications

Courtland Whited
MIS Director

Michael Creed
Network Administrator

Barbara Kesel
Head Writer

Bart Sears
Art Director

Pam Davies
Production Director

Sylvia Bretz
Janet Bechtle
Production Assistants

Michelle Pugliese
Freelance Coordinator

Michael Atiyeh
Karla Barnett
Tony Bedard
Amber Boonyaratapalin
Jim Cheung
Andrew Crossley
Frank D'Armata
Charles Decker
John Dell
Laura DePuy
Andrea Di Vito
Steve Epting
Fabrizio Fiorentino
Drew Geraci
Butch Guice
Don Hillsman II
Morry Hollowell
Rob Hunter
Tammy Jackson
Jeff Johnson
Jason Lambert
Greg Land
Ron Marz
Steve McNiven
David Meikis
Karl Moline
Tiffany Moncada
Paul Pelletier
Mark Pennington
Brandon Peterson
Justin Ponsor
James Rochelle
Caesar Rodriguez
Matt Ryan
Rob Schwager
Tom Simmons
Andy Smith
John Smith
Beth Widera